THE LIFE & ADVENTURES OF
ROBINSON CRUSOE

THE LIFE & ADVENTURES OF
ROBINSON CRUSOE

DANIEL DEFOE

JAICO PUBLISHING HOUSE

Ahmedabad Bangalore Bhopal Chennai
Delhi Hyderabad Kolkata Lucknow Mumbai

Published by Jaico Publishing House
A-2 Jash Chambers, 7-A Sir Phirozshah Mehta Road
Fort, Mumbai - 400 001
jaicopub@jaicobooks.com
www.jaicobooks.com

© Jaico Publishing House

THE LIFE & ADVENTURES OF
ROBINSON CRUSOE
ISBN 81-7224-894-6

First Jaico Impression: 2002
Sixth Jaico Impression: 2010

Printed by
Anubha Printers, B-48, Sector-7, Noida

THE LIFE AND ADVENTURES OF ROBINSON CRUSOE

I was born in the year 1632, in the city of York, of a good family. My father was a foreigner from Bremen, while my mother's relations were named Robinson. I was called Robinson Kreutznaer, but by the usual corruption of words in England we are now called Crusoe.

I had two elder brothers, one of whom was killed in battle against the Spaniards, and what became of the second I never knew. Being the third son of the family, and not having been apprenticed to any trade, my head began to be filled very early with thoughts of going abroad. My father wished

I would be satisfied with nothing but going to sea.

me to take up a career in law, but I would be satisfied with nothing but going to sea. My father, a wise and grave man, gave me

serious and excellent counsel against what
he foresaw was my design. He called me one
morning into his chamber, where he was
confined by the gout, and asked me what
reasons more than a mere wandering inclination I had for leaving my father's house
and my native country, where I had a
prospect of raising my fortune by application
and industry, with a life of ease and pleasure. He went on to point out that ours was
the middle state in life, we being neither rich
nor poor. The middle state was the best state
in the world, the most suited to human
happiness, and had the fewest disasters, as
compared to the many vicissitudes to which
the higher or lower part of mankind was
exposed. My father indicated that he would
do very kind things for me if I would stay
and settle at home as he directed. Finally, he
told me I had my elder brother for an
example, to whom he had used the same

My father warned me.

rnest persuasions to keep him from going
to war, but in vain. He warned me that if
lid take the foolish step of going to sea, I
ould have myself to blame when there

might be none to render me help. By the end of his speech, tears were running down my father's face.

I was sincerely affected with this discourse, as indeed who could not be? I resolved not to think of going abroad any more, but to settle at home according to my father's desire. But alas! a few days wore it all of, and soon I had resolved to run away from home. Thinking that my mother would be more pliable, I begged her to secure my father's consent to my going to sea at least for one voyage. But she became very agitated, and said she would not have a hand in my destruction. I learnt afterwards that she did report our conversation to my father, who affirmed that he could not give consent to my choice of a life of misery.

It was not till almost a year after this that I broke loose. I was one day at Hull, where I went casually, and without any

*As the storm increased I blamed myself
more and more.*

purpose of making an elopement that time.
One of my companions was going by sea to
London in his father's ship. He asked me to

join him, saying it would cost me nothing for my passage. I consulted neither father nor mother any more, nor so much as sent them word of it; but leaving them to hear of it as they might, without asking God's blessing or my father's, without any consideration of circumstances or consequences, and in an ill hour, God knows, on the first of September 1651, I went on board a ship bound for London.

Never any young adventurer's misfortunes, I believe, began sooner, or continued longer than mine. The ship had no sooner gotten out of the Humber, when the wind began to blow, and the waves to rise in a most frightful manner. As I had never been at sea before, I was very sick in body, and terrified in my mind. As the storm increased, I blamed myself more and more for what I had done, and for not having listened to my father's good counsel. But the next day the

I expected the ship to sink any moment.

storm subsided, and I found myself no more seasick but very cheerful. Later that night I got drunk with my companions, drowned all my repentance, and entirely forgot the vows and promises I had made while the storm raged. But I was to have yet another trial.

On the sixth day of our voyage we laid anchor near Yarmouth. We should have sailed up the river, but the wind blew very hard. Then, after eight days at anchor, a storm broke, and it was a terrible storm indeed. I began to see terror and amazement in the faces even of the seamen themselves. We had a good ship, but she was deep loaded, and wallowed in the sea. The storm was so violent, that I saw what is not often seen, the master, the boatswain, and some others more sensible than the rest, at their prayers, and expecting every moment when the ship would go to the bottom. Then, in the middle of night, the ship sprang a leak, and water collected in the hold. The master fired guns for help, and a boat from a nearby ship came to our rescue. With great hazard, we got into the boat, and, after tossing about for a while, somehow reached the shore and walked on foot to Yarmouth.

If I then had the sense to go back home, I would have been happy, and my father might even have killed the fatted calf for me. But my ill fate pushed me on now with an obstinacy that nothing could resist; and though I had several times loud calls from my reason and my more composed judgement to go home, yet I had no power to do it. I know not what to call this, nor do I know if it is a secret overruling decree that hurries us on to be the instruments of our own destruction, even though it be before us, and that we rush upon with our eyes open.

Even my comrade's father advised me with a very grave and concerned tone: 'Young man, you ought never to go to sea any more; you ought to take this experience for a plain and visible warning, that you are not to be a seafaring man.'

I travelled to London by land; and there, as well as on the road, had many struggles with myself what course of life I should take, and whether I should go home, or go to sea. As to going home, shame opposed the best motions (Promptings) that came to my thoughts; and it immediately occurred to me how I should be laughed at among the neighbours, and should be ashamed to see, not my father and mother only, but even everybody else. In this state of life I remained some time, uncertain what measure to take, and what course of life to lead. An irresistible reluctance continued to going home, and as I stayed a while, the remembrance of the distress I had been in wore off; and, as that abated, the little motion I had in my desires to a return wore off with it, till at last I quite laid aside the thoughts of it, and looked out for a voyage.

I went on board a vessel bound for the

I became friends with the master of the ship.

coast of Africa, or as our sailors commonly call it, a voyage to Guinea. On my return, I became friends with the master of a ship who had been on the coast of Guinea, and went with him on another voyage to the same country. This time I carried about £40 in such toys and trifles as the captain directed me to buy, to trade with the natives there. On this voyage, under the guidance of the captain, I got a competent knowledge of the mathematics and the rules of navigation, and learned how to keep an account of the ship's course and take an observation. In short, this voyage made me both a sailor and a merchant; for I brought home five pounds and nine ounces of gold dust, which yielded me in London at my return almost £300, and this filled me with those aspiring thoughts which have since so completed my ruin.

On my very next voyage to Guinea I fell into terrible misfortunes. Our ship, passing between the Canary Islands and the African shore, was surprised in the grey of the morning by a Turkish rover of Sallee. We were all carried as prisoners into Sallee, a

I made my getaway in a fishing boat.

port belonging to the Moors. The captain of the rover kept me as his slave, in which state I spent over two years. My plans for escape finally bore fruit, and I made my getaway in a finishing boat, taking with me a Moorish boy called Xury. We sailed along the African coast for a number of days, going ashore from time to time in search of fresh water, on which occasions we were often dreadfully frightened by the hideous cries and howlings of the wild animals. I hoped to make it to the islands of the Canaries, or to the Cape de Verde Islands, which I knew lay not far off from the coast; I knew, too, that all the ships from Europe, which sailed either to the coast of Guinea or to Brazil, or to the East Indies, made this cape, or those islands. We were finally picked up by a Portuguese ship on her way to the Brazils. In a few days' time I found myself in the Brazils, once more delivered from the most miserable of all conditions of life; and what to do next with myself, I was now to consider.

I bought some land and set up as a planter. In less than four years I was

I bought some land and set up as a planter.

beginning to thrive and prosper very well upon my plantation, and seemed all but settled in this new life. Had I continued in the station I was now in, I would have had room for all the happy things to have yet befallen me for which my father so earnestly recommended a quiet, retired life. But other things attended me, and I was still to be the wilful agent of all my own miseries. I reflected that I had gotten into an employment quite remote to my genius, and directly contrary to the life I delighted in, and for which I forsook my father's house, and broke through all his good advice; nay, I was coming into the very middle station which my father advised me to before; and which, if I resolved to go on with, I might as well have stayed at home, and never have fatigued myself in the world as I had done. And I often said to myself, I could have done this as well in England among my friends, as have gone 5,000 miles off to do it among strangers and savages.

In this manner I began to look upon my condition with the utmost regret. I happened

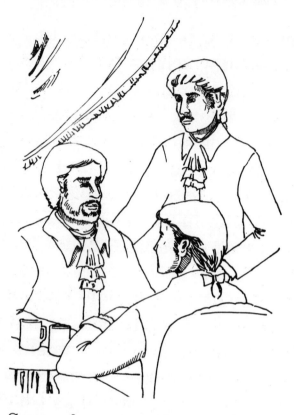

*Some of my acquaintances came
to me with a proposal.*

that some merchants and planters of my acquaintance came to me with the proposal of making a voyage to Guinea to bring back negroes as servants, as we were all straightened for nothing so much as servants to work on our plantations. At this time I could scarce have failed to be worth three or four thousand pounds sterling, with that too increasing. For me to think of a voyage to Guinea was the most preposterous thing that ever man, in such circumstances, could be guilty of. But I, that was born to be my own destroyer, could no more resist the offer than I could restrain my first designs for voyaging, when my father's good counsel was lost upon me. I agreed to go, and made a formal will, disposing of my plantations and effects, in case of my death. Had I used half as much prudence to judge what I ought to have done and not to have done, I would certainly never have gone away from so prosperous an undertaking. But I was hurried on, and obeyed blindly the dictates of my fancy rather than my reason. And accordingly, the ship being fitted out, and the cargo furnished, I went on board in an evil hour, the first of September 1659, being the same day eight years earlier than I went from my father and mother at Hull.

We passed the line (The line: the equator) in about twelve days' time, and were, by our last observation, in 7 degrees 22 minutes northern latitude, when a violent tornado, or hurricane, took us quite out of our knowledge. It left our ship leaky and very much disabled, and we decided to change course and head for the Carribee islands to get some assistance. In the latitude of 12 degrees 18 minutes a second storm came upon us, and carried us away westward, until the ship struck upon a sand. We knew nothing where we were, or upon what land it was we were driven, whether an island or the main, whether inhabited or not inhabited. In the midst of the storm, we got into a small boat, and headed towards land. What the shore was, whether rock or sand, whether steep or shoal, we knew not we only hoped that we might happen into some bay or gulf, or the mouth of some river. But, as we made nearer and nearer the shore, the land looked more frightful than the sea.

A raging wave, mountain-like, came rolling astern of us, and swallowed us all up in a moment. Having driven me, or rather carried me, a vast way on towards the shore, and having spent itself, the wave went back, and left me upon the land almost dry, but half dead with the water I took in. I got upon my feet, and endeavoured to make on towards the land as fast as I could, before another wave should return and take me up again. But the sea came pouring in after me, and twice more I was lifted up by the waves and carried forwards as before, the shore being very flat. The last time of these two had well near been fatal to me; for the sea

*As we made nearer the shore, the land looked
more frightful than the sea.*

landed me, or rather dashed me, against a
piece of rock, and that with such force, as it
left me senseless, and indeed helpless. But

I recovered a little before the return of the waves, and the next run I took I got to the mainland, clambered up the cliffs of the shore, and sat me down upon the grass, free from danger and quite out of the reach of the water.

I walked about on the shore, lifting up my hands, and my whole being, as I may say, wrapt up in the contemplation of my deliverance, marking a thousand gestures and motions which I cannot describe, reflecting upon all my comrades that were drowned, and that there should not be one soul saved but myself; for, as for them, I never saw them afterwards, except three of their hats, one cap, and two shoes that were not fellows.

I cast my eyes to the stranded vessel. I could hardly see it, the surf and the froth of the sea being so big. It lay so far off. 'Lord!' I said to myself. 'How was it possible I could get on shore?'

At the next run I took, I got to the mainland.

After I had solaced my mind with the comfortable part of my condition, I began to look round me to see what kind of place I was in, and what was next to be done, and I soon found my comforts abate, and that, in a word, I had a dreadful deliverance; for I was wet, had no clothes to shift me, nor anything either to eat or drink to comfort me, neither did I see any prospect before me but that of perishing with hunger, or being devoured by wild beasts; and that which was particularly afflicting to me was, that I had no weapon either to hunt and kill any creature for my sustenance, or to defend myself against any other creature that might desire to kill me for theirs. In a word, I had nothing about me but a knife, a tobacco-pipe, and a little tobacco in a box. This was all my provision; and this threw me into terrible agonies of mind, that for a while I ran about like a mad man.

Night coming upon me, I began to wonder if I might become a prey to a ravenous beast. I decided to get up into a thick bushy tree like a fur, but thorny, which grew near me,

I decided to get up into a thick, bushy tree.

and to sit there all night, and consider the next day what death I should die. I walked about a furlong from the shore, to see if I could find any fresh water to drink, which

I did, to my great joy; and having drunk, and put a little tobacco in my mouth to prevent hunger, I went to the tree, and getting up into it, endeavoured to place myself so, as that if I should sleep I might not fall; and having cut me a short stick, like a truncheon, for my defence, I took up my lodging, and having been excessively fatigued, I fell fast asleep.

When I awoke it was broad day, the weather clear, and the storm abated. But that which surprised me most was, that the ship was lifted off in the night from the sand where she lay, by the swelling of the tide, and was driven up almost as far as the rock where I had been so bruised by the dashing me against it. This being within about a mile from the shore where I was, and the ship seeming to stand upright still, I wished myself on board, that, at least, I might save some necessary things for my use.

*I could come within a quarter
of a mile of the ship.*

A little after noon I found the sea very
clam, and the tide ebbed so far out, that I
could come within a quarter of a mile of the

ship. My grief was renewed when I saw that, if we had remained on board, we would have all been safe, and that is to say, got safe on shore, and I would not have been left entirely destitute of comfort and company. This forced tears from my eyes again; but as there was little relief in that, I resolved, if possible, to get to the ship. So I pulled off my clothes, for the weather was hot to extremity, and took to the water. But when I came to the ship, I did not know how to get on board; for as she lay aground, and high out of the water, there was nothing within my reach to hold of. I swam round her twice, and the second time I spied a small piece of a rope, which I wondered I did not see at first, hang down by the fore-chains so low that I got hold of it, with great difficulty, and got up into the forecastle of the ship. Here I found that there was a great deal of water in her hold, but all her quarter was free, and all

*I filled my pockets with biscuits
and also ate it.*

that was in that part was dry. And first I
found that all the ship's provisions were dry
and untouched by water; and being very

well-disposed to eat, I went to the bread-room, and filled my pockets with biscuit, and ate it as I went about other things, for I had no time to lose. I also found some rum in the great cabin, of which I took a large dram, and which I had indeed need enough of to spirit me for what was before me.

I had no boat to take things ashore, so, after wondering for a while what to do, I decided to make a raft. I took some pieces of timber that I found, and cut a top-mast into smaller pieces, and put together a raft strong enough to bear any reasonable weight. My next care was what to load it with, and how to preserve what I laid upon it from the surf of the sea. After some thought, I laid all the planks and boards that I could get upon the raft, then fetched three of the seamen's chests which I had broken open and emptied, and lowered them down upon my raft. While I was filling one of these with bread, rice,

With this cargo I headed for the shore.

cheese and pieces of dried goat's flesh, I found the tide began to flow, though very calm, and had the mortification to see my coat, shirt and waistcoat, which I had left on shore upon the sand, swim away; I was left only with the breeches and the stockings that I had on me. So I rummaged for some clothes, and took no more than I wanted for present use. After long searching I found out the carpenter's chest, which was indeed a very useful prize to me, and much more valuable than shipload of gold would have been at that time. I was also keen upon securing some ammunition and arms. I took two fowling-pieces from the great cabin, and two pistols. I also took some powder-horns, a small bag of shot, two old rusty swords, and two of the three barrels of powder that were on the ship, the third having become useless due to the water. With this cargo I headed for the shore, and, going up a creek that I discovered, landed safe on shore, though not without difficulty.

My next work was to view the country and seek a proper place for my habitation.

With great labour and difficulty,
I got to the top.

Where I was, I yet knew not, whether on the continent, or on an island; whether inhabited, or not inhabited; whether in danger or wild beasts, or not. There was a hill, not above a mile from me, which rose up very steep and high, and which seemed to over top some other hills, which lay as a ridge from it, northward. I took out one of the fowling-pieces and one of the pistols, and an horn of powder; and thus armed, I travelled for discovery up to the top of that hill, where, after had with great labour and difficulty got to the top, I saw my fate to my great affliction, viz. that I was in an island environed every way with the sea, no land to be seen, except some rocks which lay a great way off, and two small islands less than this, which lay about three leagues to the west.

I found also that the island I was in was barren, and, as I saw good reason to believe, uninhabited, except by wild beasts, of whom, however, I saw none; yet I saw abundance of fowls, but knew not their kinds; neither, when I killed them, could I tell what was fit for food, and what not.

I built a hut for the night's lodging.

I came back to my raft, and fell to work to bring my cargo on shore, which took me up the rest of that day. When the night fell, I barricaded myself round with the chests and boards that I had brought on shore, and made a kind of a hut for that night's lodging.

After that, I went on board the ship almost every day. In thirteen days I visited the ship eleven times, and brought away all that one pair of hands could well be supposed to bring, though I believe verily, had the calm weather held, I should have brought the whole ship piece by piece. But preparing the twelfth time to go on board, I found the wind begin to rise. However, at low water I went on board, and though I thought I had rummaged the cabin so effectually as that nothing more could be found, yet I discovered a locker with drawers in it, in one of which I found two or three razors and one pairs of large scissors, with some ten or a dozen of good knives and forks; in another, I found about thirty-six pounds value in money, some European coin, some Brazil, some pieces of eight (Piastres), some gold, some silver.

I smiled to myself at the sight of this money. 'O drug!' (Something valueless) said I aloud, 'what art thou good for me? Thou art not worth to me; one of those knives is worth all this heap. I have no manner of use for thee; e'en remain where thou art, and go to the bottom as a creature whose life is not worth saving.' However, upon second thoughts I took it away, wrapping it all in a piece of canvas.

I got home to my little tent, where I lay with all my wealth about me very secure. I blew very hard all that night, and in the morning, when I looked out, behold, no more ship was to be seen.

My thoughts were now wholly employed about securing myself against either savages, if any should appear, or wild beasts, if any were in the island. I decided that the place I was in was not for settlement, particularly because it was upon a low moorish ground near the sea, and I believed would not be wholesome; and more particularly because there was no fresh water near it. So I resolved to find a more healthy and more convenient spot of ground.

I consulted several things in my situation, which I found would be proper for me. First, health and fresh water, I just mentioned. Secondly, shelter from the heat of the sun. Thirdly, security from ravenous creatures, whether men or beasts. Fourthly, a view to the sea, that if God sent any ship in sight I might not lose any advantage for my deliverance, of which I was not willing to banish all my expectation yet.

I found a place on the rocky side of a rising hill that satisfied all these requirements, and built a dwelling by means of wooden stakes and cables. I built a fence so strong, that neither man nor beast could get into it, or over it. The entrance into this

*I chose a place on the rocky side
of a rising hill*

place I made to be not by a door, but by a
short ladder to go over the top; which ladder,
when I was in, I lifted over after me, and so

I was completely fenced in, and fortified, as I thought, from all the world, and consequently slept secure in the night, which otherwise I could not have done.

Into this fence of fortress, with infinite labour, I carried all my riches, all my provisions, ammunition and stores. I made me a large tent, and brought into it all my provisions, and everything that would spoil by the wet; and having thus enclosed all my goods, I made up the entrance, which, till now, I had left open, and so passed and repassed, as I said, by a short ladder.

When I had done this, I began to work my way into the rock; and bringing all the earth and stones that I dug down out through my tent, I laid them up within my fence in the nature of a terrance, that so it raised the ground about a foot and a half; and thus I made me a cave just behind my tent, which served me like a cellar to my house.

I thus made a cave just behind my tent.

It cost me much labour, and many days, before all these things were brought to perfection. During this time there came a rain-storm, with a sudden flash of lightning, and after that a great clap of thunder. I was not so much surprised with the lighting, as I was with a thought which darted into my mind as swift as the lightning itself. O my powder! My very heart sank within me when I thought, that at one blast all my powder might be destroyed, on which, not my defence only, but the providing me food, as I thought, entirely depended.

Such impression did this make upon me, that after the storm was over I laid aside all my works, my building, and fortifying, and applied myself to make bags and boxes to separate the powder, and to keep it a little and a little in a parcel, and to keep it so apart, that it should not be possible to make one part fire another. I finished this work in about a fortnight, and I think my powder, which in all was about 240 pounds weight, was divided in not less than a hundred parcels. As to the barrel that had been wet,

I went out at least once every day with my gun.

I did not apprehend any danger from that, so I placed it in my new cave, which in my fancy I called my kitchen.

In the interval of time while this was

doing, I went out once, at least, every day with my gun, to see if I could kill anything fit for food. I discovered that there were goats on the island; they were shy and swift of foot, but I found that I could shoot them by climbing upon the rocks above them, when they were in the valleys.

It was, by my account, the 30th of September when I first set foot upon the island, when the sun being to us in its autumnal equinox, was almost just over my head, for I reckoned myself by observation, to be in the latitude of 9 degrees 22 minutes north of the line. After I had been on the island about ten or twelve days, it came into my thoughts that I should lose my reckoning of time for want of books and pen and ink, and should even forget the Sabbath days from the working days; but to prevent this, I cut it with my knife upon a large post, in capital letters; and making it into a great

I set up the cross on the shore
where I first landed.

cross, I set it up on the shore where I first landed, viz. 'I came on shore here on the 30th September 1659'. Upon the sides of this square post I cut every day a notch with my knife, and every seventh notch was as long again as that long one; and thus I kept my calendar, or weekly, monthly, and yearly reckoning of time.

I ought to note that among the many things which I brought out of the ship in the several trips which I made to it, I got several things of less value, but not all less useful to me, which I omitted setting down before; as in particular, pens, ink, and paper, three or four compasses, some mathematical instruments, dials, perspectives (Telescopes), charts, and books of navigation, all which I huddled together, whether I might want them or no. Also I found three very good Bibles, and several other books, all which I carefully secured. And I must not forget that we had in the ship a dog and two cats; I carried both the cats with me; and as for the dog, he jumped out of the ship himself, and swam on shore to me the day after I went

The dog was a trusty servant to me for many years.

on shore with my first cargo, and was a trusty servant to me many years. As I observed before, I found pen, ink and paper, and I husbanded (Used sparingly) them to the utmost; and while my ink lasted, I kept things very exact; but after that was gone, I could not, for I could not make ink by any means that I could devise.

I have already described my habitation, which was a tent under the side of a rock, surrounded with a strong pale of posts, and cables; but I might now rather call it a wall, for I raised a kind of wall up against it of turfs, about two foot thick on the outside, and after some time—I think it was a year and a half—I raised rafters from it leaning to the rock, and thatched or covered it with boughs of trees and such things as I could get to keep out the rain, which I found at some times of the year very violent.

To make more room for my things, I set myself to enlarge my cave, and dug into the sandy rock, creating more room, and also a door to come out on the outside of my pale

I made me a table and a chair.

or fortification. This gave me not only egress and regress, as it were a back-way to my tent and to my store-house, but gave me room to stow my goods.

I began to think my cave or vault finished, when on a sudden a great quantity of earth fell down from the top and one side. The next day I went to work and got two shores or posts pitched upright to the top, with two pieces of boards across over each post. Setting more posts up with boards, in about a week more I had the roof secured; and the posts standing in rows served me for partitions to part my house.

And now I began to apply myself to make such necessary things as I found I most wanted, as particularly a chair and a table; for without these I was not able to enjoy the few comforts I had in the world. I could not write or eat, or do several things with so much pleasure without a table.

So I went to work; and here I must observe that I had never handled a tool in my life; secondly, I had very few tools to work with; and yet by labour, application, and contrivance, I made me a table and a chair, though it took a prodigious deal of time. I then made large shelves of the breadth of a foot and a half one over another, all along one side of my cave, to lay all my tools, nails, and iron-work; and, in a word, to separate everything at large in their places, that I might come easily at them. I knocked pieces into the wall of the rock to hang my guns and all things that would hang up; so that had my cave been to be seen, it looked like a general magazine of all necessary things; and I had everything so ready at my hand, that it was great pleasure to me to see all my goods in such order, and especially to find my stock of all necessaries so great.

And now it was when I began to keep a journal of every day's employment. I kept it as long as I could; for, having no more ink, I was forced to leave it off.

One thing that I felt the lack of parti-

I found a little bag of corn among my things.

cularly was candles; for I was obliged to go
to bed as soon as it became dark, which was
generally about seven o'clock. Then I began
to save the tallow of the goats I killed, and

*Besides, there were some twenty
or thirty stalks of rice.*

with a little dish made of clay, which I baked
in the sun, to which I added a wick of some
oakum, I made me a lamp; and this gave me

light, though not a clear steady light like a candle.

Then one day I found a little bag of corn among my things; the corn was all devoured by rats, and only husks and dust remained. Hoping to make use of the bag, I shook the husks out of it on one side of my fortification, under the rock.

It was a little before the great rains that I threw this stuff away, taking no notice of anything, and not so much as remembering that I had thrown anything there. About a month later I saw a few stalks of something green shooting out of the ground, which I fancied might be some plant I had not seen; but I was surprised, and perfectly astonished, when, after a little longer time, I saw about ten or twelve ears come out, which were perfect green barley of the same kind as our European, nay, as our English barley.

At first I thought that God had

I saw about ten or twelve ears come out which were perfect green barley.

miraculously caused this grain to grow without any help of seed sown; but later I realized that it had grown out of the remains of the bag of corn that I had emptied there.

I carefully saved the ear of this corn, and resolved to sow them all again, hoping in time to have some quantity sufficient to supply me with bread. Besides this barley, there were some twenty or thirty stalks of rice, which I preserved with the same care.

About this time there occurred an earthquake, which made me run out of my dwelling in panic, fearing that the hill may roll down upon me. I saw how vulnerable my dwelling was, and how dangerous it was to live in a cave under a rocky hill. I resolved to build me a little hut in an open place, but realized that I could not do it soon.

After the earthquake there was a dreadful hurricane, and much rain. When the rain stopped, I discovered that the hurricane had tossed the wreck of the ship very near to the shore, so that I could now walk up to her when the tide was out. All through the

I found a large tortoise or turtle.

month of May I went almost every day to the wreck, and brought home a great deal of timber and boards, and two or three hundred weight of iron. It was enough to build a good boat, if I had known how.

Going down to the seaside one day in the middle of June, I found a large tortoise, or turtle. I found in her threescore eggs; and her flesh, which I cooked, was to me, at that time, the most savoury and pleasant that ever I tasted in my life, having had no flesh but of goats and fowls since I landed on the island.

It continued to rain, and, in the latter part of June, I became very ill. I was cold and shivering, with violent pains in my head. I lay in bed for days, eating or drinking very little. The horror of dying on this lonely island led me to believe that God was wrathful at me for my wicked life, and I became full of repentance and devotion. I took out one of the Bibles which I mentioned before, and began to read it a little every day. I remembered, too, that the Brazilians used tobacco as a remedy for all distempers. Taking out a roll of cured tobacco that I had

I also found melons upon the ground.

in one of the chests, I steeped it in some rum, of which I then drank a dose. I also burnt some tobacco, and inhaled its vapours. This unusual remedy worked, and I became well in a few days. I began walking about with my gun in my hand, a little and a little at a time, gathering up my strength after the recent sickness. This was my occupation from the 4th of July to the 14th.

I had a great desire to make a more perfect discovery of the island, and it was the 15of July that I began to take a more particular survey of the island itself. That day I went up the creek where I had brought my rafts on shore. On the bank of that stream I found meadows covered with grass; I found a great deal of tobacco, and diverse other plants, which I had no knowledge of; I saw several sugar-canes, but wild, and for want of cultivation imperfect.

The next day, the 16th, I went further up the same way, and the country became more woody than before. In this part I found different fruits, and particularly I found melons upon the ground in great abundance,

I built a small dwelling in the woods.

and grapes upon the trees. That night I went not back to my habitation, but slept in a tree; it was the first night, as I might say, I had lain away from home.

At the end of this march I came to a pleasant valley; the country appeared so fresh, so green, so flourishing that it looked like a planted garden. I surveyed that delicious vale with a secret kind of pleasure, to think that it was all my own; that I was king and lord of all this country.

Having spent three days in this journey, I came home. I would have liked to move my habitation to that pleasanter part of the island, but I was so enamoured of the place by the sea, that I cared not to abandon it. Yet I built a small dwelling in the woods; so that I fancied now I had my country house and my sea-coast house; and this work took me up to the beginning of August.

Then came the unhappy anniversary to my landing, September 30th. All that day I fasted and prayed. After the sun had gone down, I ate a biscuit-cake and a bunch of grapes, and went to bed.

I learned to divide the rainy season and the dry season, and knew the proper season to sow my barley and rice. From mid-February to mid-April, it was the rainy season; from mid-April to mid-August the dry season; from mid-August to mid-October the rainy season again; and from mid-October to mid-February the dry season again. Having found by experience the ill consequence of being abroad in rain, I sat within doors as much as possible during the wet months. I made good use of these months, and learned, by hard labour and constant application, to make baskets, of which I made a great many, both to carry earth, or to carry and lay up anything as I had occasion.

I made another, longer journey inland. When I had passed where my bower, or country habitation, stood, I came within view of the sea to the west; and it being a very clear day, I fairly described land, whether an island or a continent I could not tell; but it lay very high, extending from the west to the WSW at a very great distance; by my guess, it could not be less than fifteen or twenty leagues off.

I could not tell what part of the world this might be, otherwise than that I knew it must be part of America, and, as I concluded, by my observations, must be near the Spanish dominions, and perhaps was all inhabited by savages, where, if I should have landed, I would have been in a worse condition than I was now, I quieted my mind with this, and left afflicting myself with fruitless wishes of being there.

Besides, after some reflection, I came to the conclusion that if this land was the Spanish coast, I should certainly, one time or other, see some vessel pass or repass one way or other; but if not, then it was the savage coast between the Spanish country

I knew it must be part of America.

and Brazils, which are indeed the worst of savages; for they are cannibals or man-eaters, and fail not to murder and devour all the human bodies that fall into their hands.

I walked further in a leisurely fashion. I found that side of the island, where I now was, much pleasanter than mine. I saw numerous parrots and caught one, so as to take it home. I reaches the seashore on that side of the island, and found it to be far superior, with infinite number of fowls, and innumerable turtles.

I took another way to come back, but lost my way, and had to return to the seaside and then come back the way I had gone. On the way back I caught a young kid, and brought it home; for it was my hope to raise a breed of tame goats, which might supply me when my powder and shot were spent.

After returning home, I rested and regaled myself, and spent much time on the weighty affair of making a cage for my Poll. The rainy season of the autumnal equinox was now come, and I kept the 30th of September in the solemn manner as before, being the

On the way back, I caught a young kid.

second anniversary of my landing on the island.

Thus I began my third year; and though I have not given the reader the trouble of so particular an account of my works this year as the first, yet in general it may be observed, that I was very seldom idle, but having regularly divided my time, according to the several daily employments that were before me, such as, first, my duty to God, and the reading of the Scriptures; secondly, the going abroad with my gun for food, which generally took up three hours every morning, when it did not rain; the ordering, curing, preserving and cooking what I had killed or caught for my supply; these took up the greater part of the day; also, it is to be considered that the middle of the day, when the sun was in the zenith, the violence of the heat was too great to stir out; so that about four hours in the evening was all the time I could be supposed to work in, with this exception, that sometimes I changed my hours of hunting and working, and went to work in the morning, and abroad with my gun in the afternoon.

In the months of November and December, I was expecting my crop of barley and rice. But goats and hares started to eat it up; so that I had to build a hedge with a great deal of toil. Then birds descended upon the crop, and I had to kill a few and hang them up, which scared the rest for good. In the end, I gathered about two bushels of rice, and above two bushels and a half of barley, that is to say, by my guess, for I had no measure at that time. I resolved not to taste any of this crop, but to preserve it all for seed against the next season, and, in the meantime, to employ all my study and hours of working to accomplish this great work of providing myself with corn and bread; for I neither knew how to grind or make meal of my corn, or indeed how to clean it and part it; nor if made into meal, how to make bread of it and if how to make it, yet I knew not how to bake it.

It might be truly said, that now I worked for my bread. 'Tis a little wonderful, and what I believe few people have thought much upon, viz. the strange multitude of little things necessary in the providing, producing, curing, dressing, making, and finishing this one article of bread.

All the while I was at work, I diverted myself with talking to my parrot, and teaching him to speak, and I quickly taught him to know his own name, and at last to speak it out pretty loud, 'Poll', which was the first word I ever heard spoken in the island by any mouth but my own.

I now embarked upon the making of some earthen vessels, which indeed I wanted sorely. With great difficulty, I could not make above two large earthen ugly things (I cannot call them jars) in about two months' labour. I also made several smaller things with better success; such as little round pots

*I embarked upon the making of
some earthen vessels.*

and flat dishes. Then, after much effort, I
improvised a kiln and burnt hardened some
pots; so that I could put them on fire, and
boil me some meat, and make a broth.

My next concern was to get me a stone mortar to beat some corn in; but in this I failed utterly, and had to be content with making some sort of a mortar out of wood. The next difficulty was to make a sieve for separating the grain from the bran and the husk. This was a most difficult thing; but here I found some pieces of calico or muslin that I had brought from the ship, and of these I made three small sieves. The baking part was the next thing to be considered; again, after much effort, I created some sort of an oven, and baked my barely-loaves, and became, in little time, a pastry-cook into the bargain; for I made myself several cakes of the rice and puddings.

It need not be wondered at, if all these things took up most part of the third year of my abode here. All this while the thought of escaping from the island never left my mind. Then I went and looked at our ship's

*I made myself several cakes
of the rice and puddings.*

boat, which was blown up upon the shore a
great way, in the storm, when we were first
cast away. But the boat was turned almost

bottom upward, and, try as I might, I could no more set her upright than I could remove the island. Then I took it into my head to make myself a canoe, out of the trunk of a great tree. I knew the same difficulty of moving and transporting it to the sea would arise after I had it made; and yet, like a fool, I said to myself, 'Let's first make it; I'll warrant I'll find some way or other to get it along when 'tis done.' The eagerness of my fancy prevailed, and to work I went. I felled a great tree, and carved a boat out of it with infinite labour. But in the end, all my devices to get it into the water failed, though they cost me infinite labour too. This grieved me heartily.

In the middle of this work I finished my fourth year in this place. I had now been here so long, that many things which I brought on shore for my help were either quite gone, or very much wasted, and near spent. My ink, as I observed, had been gone

*All the devices to get the boat
into the water failed.*

for some time, all but a very little, which I
eked out with water, a little and a little, till
it was so pale it scarce left any appearance
of black upon the paper.

The next thing to my ink's being wasted, was that of my bread; I mean the biscuit, which I brought out of the ship. This I had husbanded to the last degree, allowing myself but one cake of bread a day for above a year; and yet I was quite without bread for near a year before I got any corn of my own.

My clothes began to decay too, mightily. Though it is true that the weather was so violent hot that there was no need of clothes, yet I could not go quite naked, no, even if I had been inclined to it, which I was not, nor could abide the thought of it, though I was all alone.

The reason why I could not go quite naked was, I could not bear the heat of the sun so well when quite naked as with some clothes on; with a shirt on, the air itself made some motion, and whistled under that shirt, was twofold cooler than without it. No more could I ever bring myself to go out in the heat of the sun without a cap or a hat.

I made me a suit of clothes wholly of skins.

I had among my things several thick watch-coats (Thick coats worn by sailors when on watch) of the seamen, but they were too hot to wear; I cut them up, and made three new waist-coats. Then, from the skins of the creatures I had killed, I made a great cap for my head, with the hair on the outside, to drive away the rain. After this I made me a suit of clothes wholly of these skins, that is to say, a waistcoat and breeches open at knees, and both loose, to keep me cool. I must not omit to acknowledge that they were wretchedly made, for if I was a bad carpenter, I was a worse tailor.

After this I spent a great deal of time and pains to make me an umbrella. I spoiled two or three, before I made one to my mind, one that could be opened and closed without great difficulty.

I cannot say that after this, for five years, an extraordinary thing happened to me. Apart from my daily routine, I devoted my time to the making of another canoe, one much smaller than the one I had made earlier. Then, by digging a canal to it of six

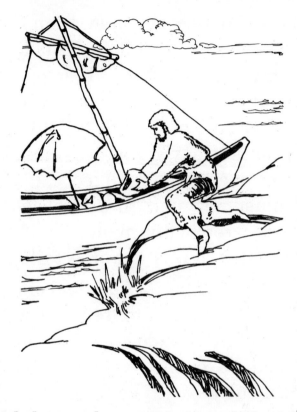

I decided to make a tour around the island.

foot wide and four foot deep, I brought it into the creek. The smallness of my boat ruled out the prospect of using it to escape from the island for good. I decided to use it to

make a tour round the island, for I was
indeed very eager to see other parts of the
coast.

I fitted the boat with a mast and a sail,
fixed my umbrella also in a step at the stern,
and made other provisions. Every now and
then I made a little excursion upon the sea,
but never went far out. Then, being eager to
view the circumference of my little kingdom,
I decided upon a long tour.

It was the 6th of November, in the sixth
year of my reign, or my captivity, if you
please, that I set out on this voyage. While
sailing around a point, my boat was caught
up in a strong current, and drifted far away
from the island. I began to give myself up for
lost; for I saw no prospect before me but of
perishing for hunger on the wide sea.

Now I looked back upon my desolated
solitary island as the most pleasant place in
the world, and all the happiness my heart

With my gun and umbrella I marched towards my dwelling.

could wish for was to be but there again. I stretched out my hands to it, with eager wishes. 'O happy desert!' said I, 'I shall never see thee more.'

But after a while, a favourable breeze began to blow, which helped me steer the boat towards the island again. About five o'clock in the evening I came within a mile of the shore, where, it being smooth water, I soon got to land. I then found a convenient bay to keep my boat, and, with my gun and umbrella, marched towards the dwelling I had built in the woods, or my country house.

I was weary, and fell asleep as soon as I lay down. I was woken out of sleep by a voice calling me by my name: 'Robin, Robin, Robin Crusoe, poor Robin Crusoe! Where are you, Robin Crusoe? Where are you? Where have you been?'

At first I thought I was dreaming, but, when I realized that the voice was real, I was dreadfully frightened, and started up in consternation. No sooner were my eyes open, then I saw my Poll sitting on the top of the hedge. It was he who had been repeating

I trapped some wild goats.

what I had talked to him, and taught him, and which he had learned so perfectly.

However, even though I knew it was the parrot, and that indeed it could be nobody else, it was a good while before I could compose myself. Also, I was amazed how the creature had got thither from my dwelling under the hill, and then, how he should just keep about the place, and nowhere else.

I perfected my method of making earthenware, and contrived to make them with a wheel. I was thus able to make tobacco-pipe. And though it was a very ugly, clumsy thing when it was done, I think I was never more vain of my own performance, or more joyful for anything I found out.

Being now in the eleventh year of my residence, and finding my ammunition growing low, I decided to tame and raise some goats, as I might not be able to kill wild ones in the near future. I trapped some wild goats, and kept them inside a fence that I built with much labour. In about a year and a half I had a flock of about twelve goats, kids and all; and in two years more I had

Like a king I dined, attended by my servants.

three and forty, besides several that I took and killed for food.

Now I not only had goat's flesh to feed on when I pleased, but milk too. I, that had never milked a cow, much less a goat, or seen butter and cheese made, very readily and handily, though after a great many essays (Attempts) and miscarriages, made me both butter and cheese at last, and never lacked it afterwards.

It would have made a stoic smile, to have seen me and my little family sit down to dinner. There was my majesty, the prince and lord of the whole island; I had the lives of all my subjects at my absolute command. I could hang, draw (Tear asunder : legal penalty for traitors), give liberty, and take it away; and no rebels among my subjects.

Then to see how like a king I dined, too, all alone, attended by my servants. Poll, as if he had been my favourite, was the only person permitted to talk to me. My dog, who had now grown very old and crazy, and had found no species to multiply his kind upon, sat always at my right hand, and two cats, one on one side of the table, and one on the other, expecting now and then a bit from my hand, as a mark of special favour.

Now I had, as I may call it, two plantations in the island; one, my little fortification or tent, with the wall about it, under the rock, with the cave behind me, which, by this, time, I had enlarged into several apartments or caves, one within another. Near this dwelling of mine, upon lower ground, lay my two pieces of corn ground, which I kept duly cultivated and sowed; and which duly yielded me their harvest in its season; and whenever I had occasion for more corn, I had more land adjoining as fit as that.

Besides this, I had my country seat, and I had now a tolerable plantation there also. Here I kept the trees always so cut, that they might spread and grow thick, and make the more agreeable shade. Under my tent here, I had made me a squab or couch, with the skins of the creatures I had killed, and with other soft things, and a blanket laid on them and a great watch-coat to cover me; and here, whenever I had occasion to be absent from my chief seat, I took up my country habitation.

Adjoining to this I had my enclosures for my cattle, that it is to say, my goats. In this place also I had my grapes growing, which I principally depended upon for my winter store of raisins, and which I never failed to preserve very carefully, as the best and most agreeable dainty of my whole diet.

As this country seat was about half-way between my other habitation and the place where I had laid up my boat, I generally stayed here on my way thither; for I frequently visited my boat, and went out in her on short excursions to divert myself. But now I come to a new scene in my life.

It happened one day, about noon, going

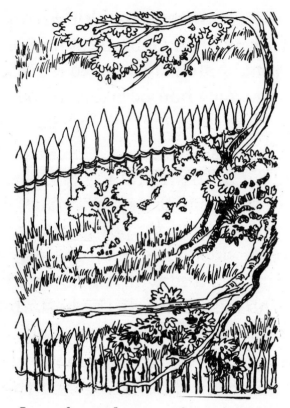

I made enclosures for my goats.

towards my boat, I was exceedingly surprised with the print of a man's naked foot on the shore, which was very plain to be seen in the sand. I stood like one thunderstruck, or as if I had seen an apparition. I listened, I looked round me, I could hear nothing, nor see anything. I went up to a rising ground, to look farther. I went up the shore, and down the shore, but it was all one; I could see no other impression but that one. I went to it again to see if there were any more, and to observe if it might not be my fancy; but there was no room for that, for there was exactly the very print of a foot—toes, heel, and every part of a foot. How it came thither I knew not, nor could in the least imagine. But after innumerable fluttering thoughts, I came home to my fortification, terrified to the last degree, looking behind me at every two or three steps, mistaking every bush and tree, and fancying every stump at a distance to be man. When I came to my castle, for so I think I called it ever after this, I fled into it like one pursued.

I slept none that night. I formed nothing

*I was exceedingly surprised by
the print of a man's foot.*

but dismal imaginations to myself. Sometimes I fancied it must be the devil; but,
after considering why the devil should leave

a single footprint; it did not seem credible. I presently concluded that it must be some of the savages of the mainland, who had wandered out to sea in their canoes, and, driven by the currents or by contrary winds, had briefly touched the island. I was very thankful in my thoughts that I was not thereabouts at that time. But perhaps they had found my boat, and knew that there were people here; they would come again in greater numbers, and devour me; if they did not find me, they would find my enclosure, destroy all my corn, carry away all my flock of tame goats, and I would perish at last for mere want.

How strange a chequer-work is the life of man! I, whose only affliction was that I seemed banished from human society, now trembled at the very apprehensions of seeing a man, and was ready to sink into the ground at but the shadow of a man's having set his foot on the island!

I had not stirred out of my castle for three days.

It came into my thought that all this might be a mere chimera of my own; and that this foot might be the print of my own foot, when I came on shore from my boat.

This cheered me up a little, and I began to persuade myself it was all a delusion; why might not I come that way from the boat? I could by no means tell, for certain, where I had trod, and where I had not.

Now I began to take courage, and to peep about again, for I had not stirred out of my castle for three days and nights. I began to go abroad again, and went down to my country house to milk my goats.

But I could not persuade myself fully until I should go down to the shore again, and see this print of a foot, and measure it by my own. But when I came to the place, first, it appeared evidently to me, that when I laid up my boat, I could not possibly be on shore anywhere thereabout; secondly, when I came to measure the mark with my own foot, I found my foot not so large by a great deal. Both these things filled my head with new imaginations; so that I shook with cold, like

I planted stakes, which grew very readily.

one in an ague. I went home again. And what course to take for my security, I knew not.

I went to work and put up a second wall round my dwelling; this outer wall I thickened with pieces of timber, old cables, and anything I could think of; and in it I made seven little holes, and through the seven holes I contrived to plant the seven muskets I had gotten from the ship.

I planted stakes, which grew very readily, all around my dwelling, so that in two years' time I had a thick grove; in a few more years, it would be so monstrous thick as to be perfectly impassable. I now used two ladders to enter my fortification; when the two ladders were taken down, no man living could come down to me without injuring himself; and if any had come down , they were still on the outside of my outer wall.

At the same time, I removed a part of my flock of goats to the remotest and most secluded part of the island.I built a strong fence around it.

After I had thus secured one part of my little living stock, I went about the whole

I was horror-stuck to see on the shore skulls and other human bones.

island, searching for another private place to make such another depot; when, wandering more to the west point of the island than I had even done yet, and looking out of sea, I thought I saw a boat upon the sea, at a great distance. I had salvaged a perspective glass (Telescope) or two from the ship; but I had none about me at the time. So; I could not make sure if it was indeed a boat that I saw. I resolved to go no more without a perspective glass in my pocket.

When I had come down the hill to the shore, where, indeed, I had never been before, I was perfectly confounded and amazed; nor is it possible for me to express the horror of my mind at seeing the shore spread with skulls, hands, feet, and other bones of human bodies; and particularly, I observed a place where there had been a fire made, and a circle dug in the earth, like a cockpit (An enclosure for cocks to fight in), where one may suppose the savage wretches had sat down to their inhuman feastings upon the bodies of their fellow creatures.

My stomach grew sick, and I was just at
the point of fainting, when Nature discharged
the disorder from my stomach. And having
vomited with an uncommon violence, I was
a little relieved, but could not bear to stay
in the place a moment; so I climbed up the
hill again with all the speed I could make,
and walked on towards my habitation.

I kept close within my own circle for almost two years after this. I used more
caution, and kept my eyes about me; and
particularly, I was more cautious of firing
my gun, lest any of the savages being on the
island should hear it. It was, therefore, a
very good providence to me that I had furnished myself with a tame breed of goats,
that I need not hunt any more about the
woods, or shoot at them. I believe for two
years I never fired my gun once off, though
I never went out without it. I now also
carried three pistols that I had saved out of

the ship, sticking them in my goat-skin belt. Also I polished up one of the great cutlasses that I had out of the ship, and made me a belt to put it on also; so that I was now a most formidable fellow to look at when I went abroad.

I was filled with such hatred towards the cannibalizing savages that I continually dreamed of ambushing and attacking them, and killing even twenty or thirty of them at a time. But then, after much reflection, I concluded that they had their customs and their way of life, and that I was not entitled to sit in judgement of them. Also I saw that it would be foolish of me to expose myself to danger unnecessarily.

I went and removed my boat, and carried it down to the east side of the island, where I knew, by reason of the currents, the savages durst not come with their boats. Besides this, I kept myself more retired than

I continually dreamed of ambushing and attacking them.

ever. The concern that was now upon me put an end to all invention, and to all contrivances that I had laid for my future accommodations and conveniences. I had the care of my safety more now upon my hands than that of my food. I cared not to drive a nail, or chop a stick of wood now, for fear the noise I should make should be heard; and, above all, I was intolerably uneasy at making any fire, lest the smoke, which is visible at a great distance in the day should betray me.

As I was afraid to make a fire in daytime, I decided to use charcoal for my daytime cooking etc. I was cutting the branches of a tree one day, to make charcoal, when I chanced upon a natural cave in the earth, which went in a vast way. I entered the cave, and was frightened out of my wits by two broad shining eyes, which twinkled like two stars, inside the darkness of the cave. Gathering up my courage after a while, I ventured into the cave again with a firebrand in my hand. Inside lay a most monstrous, old he-goat, gasping for life; and dying of mere old age. He died, indeed, the next day.

I ventured into the cave again, with a firebrand in my hand.

The next day I came again, with six large candles, crept in through the narrow part of the cave on all fours, then found the roof rising up, I believe near twenty foot. The place was a most delightful grotto. By and by, I removed almost my entire magazine of gun-powder to this sanctuary.

I fancied myself now like one of the ancient giants, which were said to live in caves and holes in the rocks, where none could come at them; for I persuaded myself, while I was here, if five hundred savages were to hunt me, they could not find me out; or, if they did, they would not venture to attack me here.

I was now in my twenty-third year of residence in this island; and was so naturalized to this place, and to the manner of living, that could I have but enjoyed the certainty that no savages would come to the place to disturb me, I could have been content to spend the rest of my time here, even to the last moment, till I had laid me down and died , like the old goat in the cave.

My Poll lived with me for six and twenty years.

I had found many diversions and amusements now, what with my Poll, my dog, my cats, two or three households kids, and some fowls. My Poll lived with me no less than six and twenty years. How long he might live afterwards I know not, though I know they have a notion in the Brazils that they live a hundred years. Perhaps poor Poll may be alive there still, calling after poor Robin Crusoe till this day.

It was now the month of December, as I said above, in my twenty-third year; when, going out pretty early in the morning, I was surprised with seeing a flight of some fire upon the shore, at a distance from me of about two miles. It was not, I noted, on the other side of the island, where I had observed some savages had been; it was on my side of the island.

I ran back to my castle, loaded all my muskets, and put myself in a posture of defence. But I could not sit there in ignorance for long; picking up my perspective-glass, I climbed to the top of the hill, and laid me down flat on my belly on the ground.

They danced around the fire.

There on the shore were no less than nine naked savages sitting round a small fire they had made. They had two canoes with them, which they had hauled up upon the shore. They danced round the fire, and, after a while, went away on the sea, the tide now being high.

I then ran to the other side of the island,and got there in less than two hours; I perceived there had been three more canoes of savages in that place; and looking out farther, I saw they were all at sea together, making over for the main. Going down to the shore, I saw the marks of horror they had left behind, viz. the blood, the bones, and part of the flesh of human bodies.

For over a year after this, I saw no more savages. But one night—the sixteenth of May it was—when a great storm was blowing outside, and I sat reading the Bible, I was surprised with a noise of a gun, as I thought, fired at sea. I started up in great haste, and climbing out of my fortification, got to the top of the hill. I heard the sound of a gun again, and knew that there was a

I went in my boat to the wreck of this ship.

ship in distress, apparently giving signals to some other ship in company. Collecting all the dry wood I could find, I started a huge fire, and kept it going all night. In the morning I saw the wreck of a ship far away. I could only make conjectures as to what had happened at sea in the course of that night, for I never saw any survivors from the ship, and this filed me with inexpressible regret, for, if but one soul had escaped to me, I might have had one companion.

I made a voyage in my boat to the wreck of this ship, and salvaged some things of use to me. I took a fire-shovel and tongs, which I wanted extremely. I also found some money in a chest, and some gold, all of which was of no use to me, but which I took away.

The disappointment I had met in the wreck I had been on board of, and where I had been so near the obtaining what I so earnestly longed for, viz. somebody to speak to, that this disappointment filled me with a great longing to sail in my boat to the mainland. I gave little thought to what would happen to me, if I fell into the hands of the savages. I was agitated wholly by my desires. All my calm of mind seemed to be suspended; and I had, as it were, no power to turn my thoughts to anything but to the project of a voyage to the mainland, which came upon me with such force, and such an impetuosity of desire, that it was not to be resisted.

I realized that I could not hope to escape on my own; but if I found a savage, who would serve me as a pilot, and tell me what to do, and where to go for provisions, and where not to go for fear of being devoured, I might certainly venture to the mainland. Thus my only way to go about an attempt for an escape was, if possible, to get a savage in my possession.

About a year and a half after I had entertained these notions, I was surprised, one morning early, with seeing no less than five canoes all on shore together on my side of the island. I soon found out, with my perspective-glass, that there were thirty savages on shore. While I was looking on them, I saw two miserable creatures being dragged from the boats. One of them was struck down, and cut open immediately for their cookery; the other, seeing a chance, ran away from them, and with incredible swiftness along the sands directly towards me, I mean towards that part of the coast where my habitation was.

I had thought that the whole crowd would pursue the escaped prisoner, but was encouraged when I saw that only three men ran in pursuit, and that too not as swiftly as the one they pursued. The savage escaping swam across the creek between them and my castle, and only two of the pursuers now followed him. I took a short cut down the hill, and positioned myself in the way between the pursuers and the pursued. At

Only two of the pursuers now followed him.

the right moment, I hit one of the pursuers with the butt of my gun, and the other I shot down.

I called the escaping savage, and made

signs inviting him to come forward, which he easily understood, and came a little way, then stopped again, and then a little further, and stopped again; and I could then perceive that he stood trembling. I beckoned him again, and gave signs of encouragement; and he came nearer and nearer, kneeling down every ten or twelve steps. I smiled at him, and looked pleasantly, and beckoned to him to come still nearer. At length he came close to me, and then he kneeled down again, kissed the ground, and laid his head upon the ground, and taking me by the foot, set my foot upon his head.

He spoke some words to me; and though I could not understand them, yet I thought they were pleasant to hear; for they were the first sound of a man's voice that I had heard, my own excepted, for above twenty-five years.

I took him, not to my castle, but quite

*He came close to me, and then
kneeled down again.*

away to my cave, on the farther part of the
island. Here I gave him bread and a bunch
of raisins to eat, and a draught of water,
which he was indeed in great distress for.

He was a comely handsome fellow, perfectly well made, with straight strong limbs, not too large, tall, and well-shaped, and, as I reckon, about twenty-six years of age. He had a very good countenance, not a fierce and surly aspect; he had all the sweetness and softness of an European in his countenance too, especially when he smiled. His hair was long and black, not curled like wool; his forehead very high and large; and a great vivacity and sparkling sharpness in his eyes. His face was round and plump; his nose small, not flat like the negroes; a very good mouth, thin lips, and his fine teeth well set, and white as ivory.

In a little time I began to speak to him, and teach him to speak to me; and, first, I made him know his name should be Friday, which was the day I saved his life. I likewise taught him to say master, and then let him know that was to be my name.

I made him a jerkin of goat's skin.

He had a great mind to eat the two savages that we had killed; but I appeared very angry, and expressed my abhorrence of it. I took him to my castle, and gave him a pair of linen drawers; then I made him a jerkin of goat's-skin, and gave him a cap. Thus he was clothed of the present tolerably well, and was mighty well pleased to see himself almost as well clothed as his master.

I made a little tent for him beside my fortifications. At night I barred up the door, taking in my ladders too. I took all weapons inside every night. But I needed not all this precaution; for never man had a more faithful, loving, sincere servant than Friday was to me.

My gun's power to kill man, beast, bird, or anything near or far off, was a source of great amazement to Friday. He would speak to my gun, and talk to it, praying to it not to kill him.

To wean him away from his cannibal nature, I gave him boiled meat of goat, and also roasted meat. He relished it exceedingly; and at last he told me he would never eat

*He told me all he knew,
with the greatest openness.*

man's flesh any more, which I was very glad to hear.

I taught him different types of work, and

in a little time he was able to do all the work for me, as well as I could do it myself.

This was the pleasantest year of all the life I led in this place. Friday began to talk pretty well, and indeed talked a great deal to me; so that I began now to have some use for my tongue again, by way of speech. I asked Friday a thousand questions about his country, its inhabitants, the sea, the coast, and what nations were near. He told me all he knew, with the greatest openness imaginable. The nations of his sort of people he named as the Caribs, from whence I easily understood that these were the Caribbees. He also told me that a great way beyond the setting of the moon there dwelt white-bearded men, whom I took to be Spaniards.

Friday told me about the god Benamuckee in whom his people believed. I endeavoured to instruct Friday in the knowledge of the

*"O glad! there see my country,
there my nation!"*

true God, and spent many hours in religious
discourse with him. I ought to admit that I
sometimes found his natural and innocent

questions hard to answer, as when he asked, 'If God much strong, much might as the devil, why God not kill the devil, so make him no more wicked do?' I was ill qualified to be a casuist, or a solver of difficulties; I had more sincerity than knowledge in this matter; yet I succeeded in my endeavour in the end. The savage was now a good Christian, a much better one than I.

One day we were standing on the top of the hill at the east side of the island. The weather being very serene, Friday looked towards the mainland on the horizon, and, in a kind of surprise, fell a-jumping and dancing. 'O joy!' said he, 'O glad! there see my country, there my nation!'

I asked him if he would not go to his own nation; he said he would , but only if I would go with him. 'I go!' says I; why, they will eat me if I come there.' No, no, says he, 'me make them no eat you; me make they much love you.' Then he told me how kind they were to seventeen white men who came on shore there in distress.

From this time I confess I had a mind to venture over and see if I could possibly join with these white men, who I had not doubt were Spaniards or Portuguese. Once I joined up with them on the mainland, it would be much easier to find some method to reach the civilized world.

I showed Friday the large boat I had made, and which I could not get into water. But it had lain unused for about two and twenty years, and was not in serviceable condition any longer. We then set about making a new boat, and in about a month's hard labour we finished it, and made it very handsome. It cost us a fortnight more to get her into the water. I then fitted her with a mast and a sail; Friday was dexterous in handling the boat, but had no experience of a sail. He was amazed to see how I worked the boat by the rudder, and how the sail shifted as the course changed.

I was now entered on the seven and twentieth year of my captivity in this place; I had an invincible impression upon my thoughts that my deliverance was at hand, and that I should not be another year upon the island. However, I went on with my husbandry, digging, planting, fencing, as usual. We made a sort of a dock for our boat, and covered her with boughs of trees, to keep the rain off; and thus we waited for the month of November and December, in which I designed to make my adventure.

When the settled season began to come in, I was preparing daily for the voyage, laying up provisions, and so on. One day I sent Friday to the seashore to get us a tortoise. He had not been long gone when he came running back, and cried out, 'O

We covered our boat with boughs of trees.

master! O master! O sorrow! O bad! I asked
him what was the matter, and he answered
that there were three canoes on the shore.
The poor fellow was terrified, thinking that

they had come to look for him, and would cut him in pieces, and eat him. I divided all my arms, muskets, fowling-pieces, and pistols, between the two of us; I hung my great sword, as usual, naked by my side, and gave Friday his hatchet.

Taking my perspective-glass, I went up the side of the hill; and I found out quickly that there were one and twenty savages, three prisoners, and three canoes, and the scene seemed to be set for a barbarous banquet. I was filled with indignation, and, in a fit of fury, made up my mind to attack the cannibals. I sent Friday up a tree, and asked him to tell me what he saw from there. Coming back, he told me that they had already killed one of the prisoners, and the next, whom, they would kill, was not one of their nation, but one of the bearded men that had come to their country in a boat. I was filled with horror at the very mention of the

I sent Friday up a tree.

white bearded man; I went up the tree myself, and saw that he was indeed an European, and had clothes on.

I had now not a moment to lose, for

nineteen of the dreadful wretches sat upon the ground, all huddled together, and had just sent the other two to butcher the poor Christian.

Hidden behind the trees, Friday and I fired simultaneously; I saw that he killed two, and wounded three more; and on my side I killed one, and wounded two. The savages were in a dreadful consternation; we fired again, and a few more fell. Then I rushed out of the wood, and showed myself, with Friday close at my foot. Running as fast as I could, I reached the poor victim, and untied him, while Friday fired at the running savages. I asked the man what countryman he was, and he said, Espagniole. I gave him a pistol and a sword, and, though weak, he was bold and brave, and joined the fight. We killed almost all the savages; only three of them got away in a boat, along with one wounded, who might have been dead.

I gave the man some rum to revive him.

Friday and I were anxious to pursue the escaping savages in a boat, but when I went to the canoe they had left behind, I was surprised to find another poor creature lie there alive, bound hand and foot. I untied him, and when Friday saw him, he at once kissed him, embraced him, cried, laughed, danced, sang, and it was a good while before I could make him speak to me, or tell me what the matter was; but when he came a little to himself, he told me that it was his father.

I gave the man some rum out of my bottle to revive him, and Friday ran and fetched water and some bread. We brought the two men, the Spaniard and Friday's father, to our fortification, and made a very handsome tent for them near it. We made them two beds of good rice-straw, with blankets laid upon it to lie on, and another to cover them, on each bed.

My island was now peopled, and I thought myself very rich in subjects; and it was a merry reflection, which I frequently made, how like a king I looked. First of all,

I began to converse with my new subjects.

the whole country was my own mere property, so that I had an undoubted right of dominion. Secondly, my people were perfectly subjected. I was absolute lord and lawgiver; they all owed their lives to me, and were ready to lay down their lives, if there had been occasion for it, for me. It was remarkable, too, we had but three subjects, and they were of three different religions. My man Friday was a Protestant, his father was a Pagan and a cannibal, and the Spaniard was a Papist. However, I allowed liberty of conscience throughout my dominions.

I began to enter into a little conversation with my two new subjects; and first, I set Friday to enquire of his father what he thought of the escape of the savages in that canoe, and whether we might expect a return of them in greater numbers. His opinion was that, if indeed they had survived the storm that blew after they went away, they were not likely to return, for they had thought that the two which appeared before them on the shore, viz. Friday and me, were two heavenly spirits, or furies, come down to destroy them; for it was impossible to them to conceive that a man could dart fire, and speak thunder, and kill at a distance without lifting up a hand, as was done now.

Yet I was under continual apprehen-sions for a good while, and kept always upon my guard, me and all my army.

In a little time, however, no more canoes appearing, the fear of their coming wore off, and I began to take my former thoughts of a voyage to the mainland into consideration; being likewise assured, by Friday's father, that I might depend upon good treatment from their nation, on his account, if I would go.

I learned from the Spaniard that there were sixteen more of his countrymen and Portuguese living amongst the savages; he told me they had some arms with them, but they were perfectly useless, for they had neither powder nor ball; he also told me that, having neither vessel, nor tools to build one, or provisions of any kind, they could not carry out any design of escape. I suggested to him that we might bring them here, and, with so many hands, build a bark large enough to carry us all away. I told him frankly that I feared their treachery if I put my life into their hands; that they might make me their prisoner in the Spanish colonies in America. He assured me that they would not do such a thing, and that, if I pleased, he would go to them with the old man, an discourse with them about it, and return again, and bring me their answer.

But then he pointed out that our provision of corn, rice etc. was not adequate to feed so many people, should they come, and that scarcity of food itself might then create discord and enmity; he suggested that we should wait another harvest, and stock up more food.

We busied ourselves cultivating more land.

I took this excellent advice, and the four of us busied ourselves cultivating more land; at the same time, I contrived to increase my flock of goats, by adding to it the kinds of wild goats that I shot; and, the season for curing grapes coming on, I laid by a prodigious quantity of raisins. At harvest-time, we brought in and thrashed out above two hundred and twenty bushels of barley, beside a large quantity of rice.

And now having a full supply of food for all the guests I expected, I gave the Spaniard leave to go over to the mainland, to see what he could do with those he had left behind him there. I gave a musket each to the Spaniard and the old savage, with some powder and ball.

This was a cheerful work, being the first measures used by me, in view of my deliverance, for now twenty-seven years and some days.

It was no less than eight days I had waited for them, when a strange and unforeseen accident intervened. I was fast asleep in my hutch one morning, when my man

"Master, master, they are come, they are come!"

Friday came running to me, and called aloud, "Master, master, they are come, they are come!"

I jumped up, and regardless of danger,

went out without my arms, which was not my custom to do. I was surprised when, turning my eyes to the sea, I presently saw a boat at about a league and an half's distance heading for the shore, with a shoulder-of-mutton sail (A triangular sail shaped like a shoulder of mutton).

I climbed up to the top of the hill with my perspective-glass, and observed a ship laying at anchor about two leagues and an half's distance from me, south-south-east. By my observation, it appeared plainly to be an English ship, and the boat appeared to be an English longboat.

I cannot express the confusion I was in; though the joy of seeing a ship, and one that I had reason to believe was manned by my own countrymen, and consequently friends, was such as I cannot describe. But yet I had some secret doubts hung about me, bidding me keep upon my guard. In the first place

The boat landed, and the men came ashore.

it occurred to me to consider what business
an English ship could have in that part of
the world, since it was not the way to or from
any part of the world where the English had

any traffic; if they were English really it was most probable that they were here upon no good design.

The boat landed, and the men came ashore. They were in all eleven men, whereof three I found were unarmed, and, as I thought, bound; and when the first four or five of them had jumped on shore, they took those three out of the boat, as prisoners. The three were treated roughly by the other men.

The fellows scattered about the land, as if they wanted to see the country. I observed that the three mother men also had liberty to go where they pleased.

The men had come ashore at the top of high water. They had carelessly stayed till the tide was spent, leaving their boat aground. They had left two men in the boat, who were drunk, and had fallen asleep.

When the men returned they tried to move the boat, but found that they could not,

I resolved to discover myself to them.

so they decided to wait till the tide came up again. I knew it would be no less than ten hours before the boat could be afloat again, and by that time it would be dark.

In the meantime, I fitted myself up for a battle, as before, though with more caution, knowing I had to do with another kind of enemy than I had at first. My figure, indeed, looked very fierce. I had my formidable goat-skin coat on, with the great cap I have mentioned, a naked sword by my side, two pistols in my belt, and a gun upon each shoulder.

It was my design not to make any attempt till it was dark; but about two o'clock, being the heat of the day, I found that they were all gone stragling into the woods, and were probably asleep. The three poor distressed men, however, were set down under the shelter of a great tree, at about a quarter of a mile from me, and out of sight of any of the rest.

Upon this I resolved to discover myself to them, and learn something of their condition. Immediately I marched in the figure as above, my man Friday at a good distance behind me, as formidable for his arms as I, but not making quite so staring a spectre-like figure as I did.

I came as near them undiscovered as I could, and then, before any of them saw me, I called aloud to them in Spanish, 'What are ye, gentlemen?'

They were so stunned that they were about to fly from me, when I spoke to them in English. 'Gentlemen,' said I, 'do not be surprised at me; perhaps you may have a friend near you, when you did not expect it.'

When they had got over the shock, I learnt their story. One of the men was the commander of the ship that lay at anchor; his men having mutinied against him, had set him on shore in this desolate place, along with two men, one being his mate, and the other a passenger.

I asked the commander if his captors had any firearms. He answered that they had

I offered to seek deliverance of the three men.

only two pieces, and one which they had left in the boat. He also told me that there were two desperadoes among them; if they were secured, he believed all the rest would return to their duty.

I offered to seek deliverance of the three men, on two conditions. *1.* While they were on the island, they would wholly and absolutely be under my authority. *2.* If the ship were recovered from the mutineers, the commander must carry me and my man to England, passage free.

He assured me earnestly, that he would comply with these most reasonable demands. I then gave each of the three a musket, and prepared for the attack.

We were fortunate to shoot and kill one of the two desperadoes, and the other was very much wounded, and then knocked down with the butt of a gun. After that, the rest of the men surrendered easily, and were bound hand and foot. Three more stragglers appeared, hearing the sound of guns; they submitted to be bound also, and so our victory was complete.

The captain and I told each other our

The captain admired my fortification.

stories, and he was much amazed at mine. I carried him and his two men into my apartment, and showed them all the contrivances I had made during my long long inhabiting

Our business now was how to regain the ship.

that place. All I showed them was perfectly amazing to them; but above all, the captain admired my fortification.

Our business now was how to regain the

ship. The captain told me that there were still six and twenty hands on board, who, having entered into a cursed conspiracy, and knowing its grave consequences, would be hardened in it by desperation; there would be therefore no attacking them with so small a number as we were.

It presently occurred to me that in a little while the ship's crew, wondering what was become of their comrades, and of the boat, would certainly come on shore in their other boat to look for them; and that they might come armed. I told the captain that the first thing to do was to stave the boat, which lay upon the beach, so that they might not carry her off; and taking everything out of her, leave her useless. Accordingly, we took away all the provisions on board, as also the oars, mast, sail and rudder. We knocked a great hole in her bottom. Then we heaved the boat up upon the beach so high that the tide would not carry her off.

While we sat musing what we should do, we heard the ship fire a gun, and saw her wave her ensign as a signal for the boat to come on board. But no boat stirred; and they fired several times, making other signals for the boat. At last we saw them, by the help of my perspective-glass, hoist another boat out, and row towards the shore; and we found, as they approached, that there were no less than ten men in her, and that they had firearms with them.

Some of our prisoners I sent with Friday to my cave, and left them bound, giving them provisions. Two were taken into my service, upon the captain's recommendations, and upon their solemnly engaging to live and die with us; so with them and the three honest men we were seven men well armed; and I had no doubt we should be able to deal well enough with the ten that were a-coming.

As soon as they got to the place where

their other boat lay, they ran their boat upon the beach, and came all on shore. It was easy to see that they were greatly surprised to find their other boat stripped of all that was in her, and a great hole in her bottom. They were so astonished that they apparently resolved to go back to the ship. But they had not been long in the boat again, when we perceived them all coming on shore again. But this time they left three men in the boat, and the rest went up into the country to look for their fellows.

This was a great disappointment to us, for now we were at a loss what to do; for our seizing those seven men on shore would be no advantage to us if we let the boat escape, because they would then row away to the ship, and then the rest of them were sure to weigh anchor and set sail, and so our hope of recovering the ship would be lost. What was worse, the three who remained in the

They sat together under a tree.

boat put her off a good distance from the shore, and came to an anchor to wait for the other seven; so that it was impossible for us to attack them in the boat.

Those that came on shore kept close together, and marched towards the top of the little hill under which my habitation lay. When they came to the brow of the hill, not caring, it seems, to venture far from the shore, they sat down together under a tree. After long consultations amongst themselves, we saw them all start up, and march down towards the sea.

It was clear that they had given up their search. The captain was in despair at the prospect of losing any chance of regaining the ship; but I presently thought of a stratagem to bring them back again.

I ordered Friday and the captain's mate to go over the little creek westward, and as soon as they came to a little rising ground, I bade them halloo as loud as they could, and wait till they found that the seamen heard them; and thus to lure them further and further away into the island, and among the woods.

We surprised the two men left with the boat.

The stratagem worked. The seven men were presently stopped by the creek, where, the water being up, they could not cross over, and called for the boat to come up and set them over, as, indeed, I expected.

When they had set themselves over, they took one of the three men out of the boat to go along with them and left only two in the boat, having fastened her to the stump of a little tree on the shore.

That was what I wished for; and immediately, leaving Friday and the captain's mate to their business, I took the rest with me, and crossing the creek out of their sight, we surprised the two men left with the boat, and took them prisoner.

It was several hours after Friday and the captain's mate came back that we heard the seven men returning. It was quite dark now, and, from their conversation, we gathered that they were exceedingly tired and footsore; which was very welcome news to us.

At length they came up to the boat; but 'tis impossible to express their confusion when they found the boat fast aground in the creek, the tide ebbed out, and their two men gone. We could hear them call to one another in a most miserable manner, telling one another they were gotten into an enchanted island.

I drew my ambuscade nearer, and ordered Friday and the captain to creep upon their hands and feet, and get as near them as was possible, before they opened fire.

They had not been long in that posture when the boatswain, who was the principle ringleader of the mutiny, and now looked the most dejected and dispirited of them all, came walking in their direction, with two more of their crew. When they came nearer, the captain and Friday let fly at them. The boatswain was killed on the spot; another fell just by him; and the third ran for it.

At the noise of the fire I immediately advanced with my whole army, which was now eight men, viz. myself, generalissimo; Friday, my lieutenant-general; the captain and his two men, and the three prisoners of war, whom we had trusted with arms.

We came upon them in the dark, so that they could not see our number. I decided to try and see if we could bring them to a parley. So I bade one of our prisoners talk to them, who told them that they were up against fifty men; and, in the end, they all laid down their arms, and begged for their lives. And then my great army of fifty men, who in reality were all but eight, came up and seized them all; only that I kept myself and one more out of sight for reasons of state.

The captain told our prisoners that the governor of the island was an Englishman, and, as he had given them quarter, he supposed he would send them to England, to be dealt with there as justice required. I retired in the dark from them, that they might not see what kind of a governor they

Finally, they surrendered, and begged for their lives.

had, and called the captain to me. When I called, one of the men was ordered to speak again, and say to the captain, 'Captain, the commander calls for you'. And presently the captain replied, 'Tell his excellency I am just a-coming.' Thus they all believed that the commander was just by with his fifty men.

In the morning I sent the captain to parley with our prisoners. He told them that, if they were sent to England they would all be hanged in chains; but that if they would join in an attempt to recover the ship, he would have the governor's formal promise for their pardon. The proposal was readily accepted by the men.

So the next night the captain went out in the two boats with some of the men, and came up to the ship about midnight. They entered the ship, overpowered the men they encountered, and managed to shoot and kill the new captain; upon which the rest yielded, and the ship was taken effectually.

As soon as the ship was secured, the captain ordered seven guns to be fired,

Next night the captain set off with the two boats.

which was the signal agreed upon with me
to give me notice of his success, which you
may be sure I was very glad to hear, having
sat upon the shore for it till near two o'clock
in the morning.

Having thus heard the signal plainly, I laid me down; I slept very sound, till I was something surprised with the noise of a gun; and presently starting up, I heard a man call me by the name of 'Governor, Governor', and presently I knew the captain's voice; when climbing up to the top of the hill, there he stood, and pointing to the ship, he embraced me in his arms. 'My dear friend and deliverer,' says he, 'there's your ship, for she is all yours, and so are we, and all that belong to her.' I cast my eyes to the ship, and there she rode just about half a mile from the shore. I was at first ready to sink down with the surprise; for I saw my deliverance, indeed, visibly put into my hands, all things easy, and a large ship just ready to carry me away whither I pleased to go.

The captain sent me many things as present, much food and drink, and especially new and very good clothes, shirts, neck-

The captain sent me many things as presents.

cloths, gloves, shoes, a hat, stockings, and a
suit; in a word, he clothed me from head to
foot.

It was a very kind and agreeable present,

as anyone may imagine, to one in my circumstances; but never was anything in the world so unpleasant, awkward, and uneasy as it was to me to wear such clothes at their first putting on.

In these new clothes, I made my appearance before all the men. I ordered that five of the worst rebels be left behind on the island, with suitable provisions. I told these men the story of the sixteen Spaniards that were to be expected, for whom I left a letter, and made the men promise to treat the Spaniards well. The next morning two of these men swam back to the ship's side, begging to be taken into the ship; after their solemn promises of amendment, they were taken on board.

When I took leave of the island, I carried on board, as relics, the great goat's-skin cap I had made, my umbrella, and my parrot; also I forgot not to take the money I formerly mentioned.

I left the island on the 19th of December.

And thus I left the island, the 19th of December, as I found by the ship's account, in the year 1686, after I had been upon it eight-and-twenty years, two months, and nineteen days.

In this vessel, after a long voyage, I arrived in England, the 11th of June, in the year 1687, having been thirty and five years absent.

When I came to England, I was as perfect a stranger to all the world as if I had never been known there. The widow, with whom I had left my money in trust, was alive, but was in poor financial circumstances. I helped her out as much as I could.

I went down afterwards to Yorkshire; but my father was dead, and my mother and all the family extinct, except that I found two sisters, and two of the children of one of my brothers. As I had been long ago given up for dead, there had been no provision made for me; so that, in a word, I found nothing to relieve or assist me.

After making several reflections upon the circumstances of my life, I resolved to go to Lisbon, and see if I might not come by some

*The old man gave me information
regarding my estate.*

information of the state of my plantation in
the Brazils, and of what had become of my
partner there, who I had reason to suppose

had some year now given me up for dead. With this view I sailed for Lisbon, accompanied by my man Friday.

In Lisbon, I found out my old friend the captain of the ship who first took me up at sea off the shore of Africa. He was grown old now, and had left off the sea. The old man gave me information regarding my estate in the Brazils, and also offered me some money, in Portuguese gold coins, being the proceeds of the sale of product from my estate. The trustees I had appointed to look after my estate had apparently discharged their duty efficiently and honestly. In due course I received a letter from my partner, congratulating me very affectionately upon my being alive, giving me an account of how the estate was improved. He invited me very passionately to come over and take possession of my property; and, in the meantime, asked for orders as to whom he should deliver my

effects, if I did not come myself. Simultaneously, I received the large quantity of
goods, viz., sugar and tobacco, that he sent
me, being the produce of my land, and the
rest of the whole account in gold.

I was now master, all of a sudden, of
above £5,000 sterling in money, and had an
estate in the Brazils of above a thousand
pounds a year.

I was now to consider which way to steer
my courst next, and what to do with the
estate that Providence had thus put into my
hands; and, indeed, I had more care upon my
head now than I had in my silent state of life
in the island, when I wanted nothing but
what I had, and had nothing but what I
wanted; whereas I had now a great charge
upon me, and my business was how to secure
it. I had ne'er a cave now to hide my money
in, or a place where it might lie without lock
or key till it grew mouldly and tarnished
before anybody would meddle with it.

For various reasons, I was not keen upon going back to the Brazils; so I resolved at last to go to England. I prepared to go there with all my wealth. Having settled my affairs, sold my cargo, and turned all my effects into good bills of exchange, my next difficulty was which way to go to England. I had been accustomed enough to the sea, and yet I had a strange aversion to going to England by sea at that time; I could give no reason for it, though it is true I had been very unfortunate by sea, and this might be some of the reason.

I was so prepossessed against my going by sea at all, except from Calais to Dover, that I resolved to travel all the way by land. So in the company of two English merchants, the son of an English merchant in Lisbon, and two Portuguese gentlemen, along with our respective servants, my man Friday included, I set out from Lisbon.

I thus set out from Lisbon.

We passed through Madrid, and came to
Pampeluna (Pamplona), where it snowed so
much that the roads were quite impassable.
However, we found a guide who undertook

to take us through the mountain passes by such ways as were not much affected by snow. On the way, we encountered a huge bear; Friday had much fun at the bear's expense, by making it climb onto a narrow branch of a tree after him; and then killed it with his gun. Later in the passes, we were attacked by packs of wolves that were attacked by packs of wolves that were famished because of the snow; the howling and yelling of those hellish creatures were terrible, and we seemed to be surrounded by them. But, by managing our fire power cleverly, we finally drove them away, and arrived in Toulouse.

I had never been more acutely aware of danger in my life; for seeing above three hundred devils come roaring and open-mouthed to devour us, and having nothing to shelter us or retreat to, I had given myself up for lost; and I shall never care to cross

I shall never care to cross
these mountains again.

those mountains again. I think I would much
rather go a thousand leagues by sea, though
I were sure to meet with a storm once a
week.

In England my principal guide and adviser was the good old widow. The thought of going to the Brazils came to my mind again, but I abandoned it. I had all my estate there sold, and received 33,000 pieces of eight (Piastres) for it.

Any one would think that in this state of complicated good fortune I was past running any more hazards; and so indeed I would have been, if other circumstances had concurred. But I was inured to a wandering life, had no family, not many relations, nor, however rich, had I contracted much acquaintance; and though I had sold my estate in the Brazils, yet I could not keep the country out of my head, and had a great mind to be upon the wing again; especially I could not resist the strong inclination I had to see my island, and to know if the poor Spaniards were still living there, and how the rogues I left there had treated them.

I visited my island, and met my successors, the Spaniards.

In the meantime, I married, and had three children; my wife died, and, one of my nephews being a seaman, I went with him on a voyage to the East Indies.

On this voyage I visited my island, saw my successors the Spaniards, had the whole story of their lives, and of the villains I left there; how at first, they insulted the poor Spaniards, and how at last the Spaniards were obliged to use violence with them, and thus to subject them. The Spaniards also told me of their battles with the Caribbeans, who landed several times upon the island; also of the improvements they made upon the island itself; and how five of them made an attempt upon the mainland, and brought away eleven men and five women prisoners, by which, at my coming, I found about twenty young children on the island.

Here I stayed about twenty days, left them supplies of all necessary things. Besides this, I shared the island into parts with them, reserved to myself the property of the whole, but gave them such parts respectively as they agreed on; and having settled all

*I settled everything with them,
and left the place.*

things with them, and made them promise
not to leave the place, left them there.

From thence I touched at the Brazils,

from whence I sent some women to the island, for wives to such as would take them. I also sent five cows, some sheep, and some hogs.

But all these things, with an account of how three hundred Carribbeans came and invaded the island, and were finally destroyed; all these things, with some very surprising incidents in some new adventures of my own, for ten more years, I may perhaps give a farther account of hereafter.